To order additional copies of this book, contact:
Xlibris
844-714-8691
www.Xlibris.com
Orders@Xlibris.com

ISBN: Softcover   978-1-6698-0095-8
         Hardcover   978-1-6698-0097-2
         EBook   978-1-6698-0096-5

Print information available on the last page.

Rev. date: 11/24/2021

Oh Those Crazy Dogs!
Colby And Teddi Bear Go To The Circus

Dedicated to Amber and Tyse

Introduction

This is a story about two crazy dogs, their adventures, and the mischief they get into. They are very loving dogs, but they can't help getting into things.

"Hi! I'm Colby! I'm big and red and furry! I love everyone but sometimes people are afraid of me because I am so big!"

"Hi! I'm Teddi Bear! I'm big and white and very funny! I'm not as big as Colby, but just about. Everyone thinks I'm cute, and I put shows on for them."

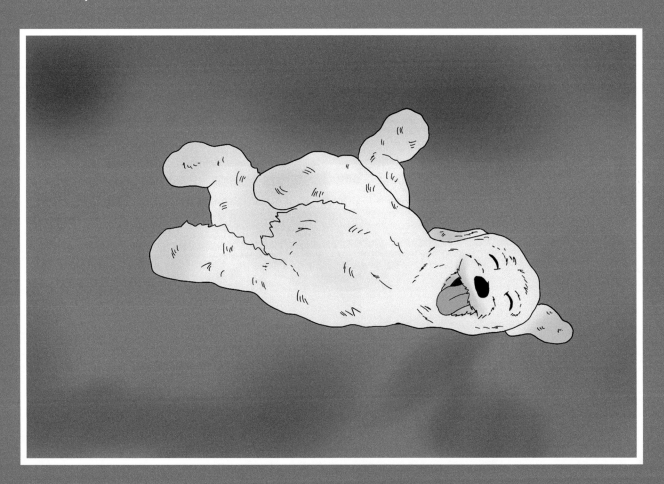

"Our owners picked us out and specially brought us home to love and care for us. We love them too, very much. They give us everything and a warm loving home. We will call them Mom and Pop.

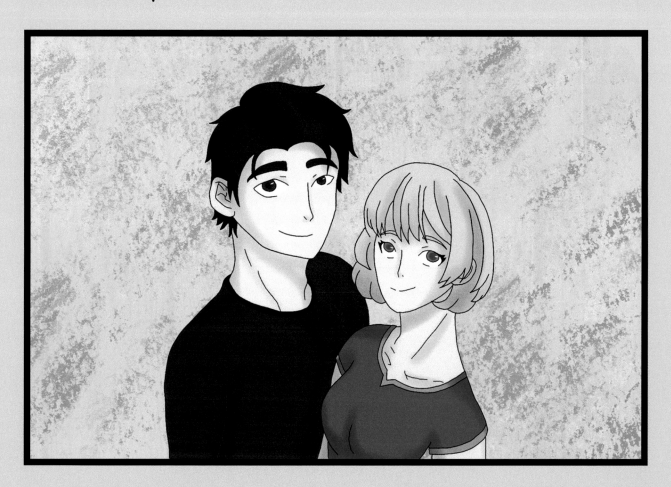

"Sometimes, we don't listen to them, especially me, Teddi Bear!"

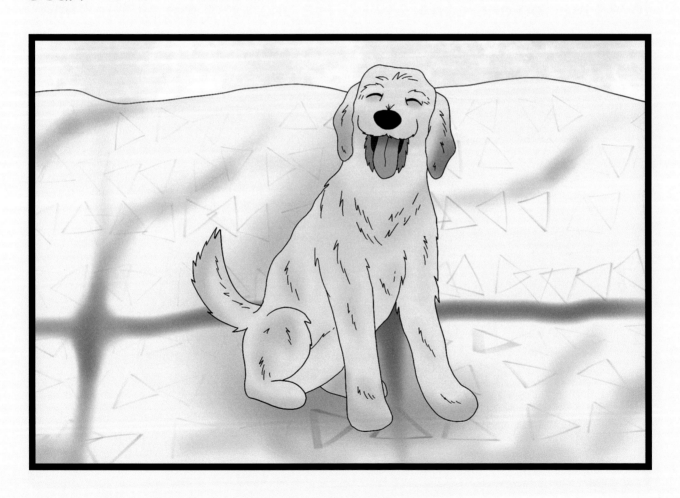

"Our mom and pop love us anyway. Sometimes, I get Colby in trouble. I can get him to do anything I want because he loves me too and can't say no. He protects me all the time."

COLBY AND TEDDI BEAR GO TO THE CIRCUS

One day, Colby and Teddi Bear were lying next to the pool. They had just had a fun time swimming and were now drying off. All of a sudden, they heard a scratching sound at the gate. Then they heard, "Psst, psst, hey, Colby, Teddi Bear."

Colby looked around. Mom had gone in the house a few minutes ago.

Colby said, "My pop put bricks under the gate, so we can't dig it up like we did last time."

"No problem," said Digger. "We'll just have to dig a hole in another spot."

"Oh," said Colby, "we better not dig anywhere that Mom has her flowers and gardens. They mean a lot to her."

"No problem," replied Digger. "You tell me where there is a place with no flowers, and we can start digging."

"Here's a spot," said Colby. "Start digging here."

"Okay," everyone said at the same time.

While they were digging, Digger asked, "Hey, guys, how would you like to take a trip to the circus?"

"The circus? What is that?" asked Colby and Teddi Bear together.

"Haven't you guys been anywhere?" asked Digger.

"Well, we have been on very long rides to go to the cottage. We have seen a lot of things on the way but not a circus. We go for long walks around the neighborhood and rides to different places with Mom and Pop," replied Colby.

"That sounds very nice, but today, you are going to the circus. It is very exciting!" said Digger.

"Hey, Digger, can we get Tyse on the way to the circus?" asked Teddi Bear.

"Yes, for sure," replied Digger.

"Tyse is really going to love it there, but how do we get him out without his mom seeing us?" asked Colby.

"I don't know," replied Teddi Bear, "but Tyse is very smart, and I bet he can find a way out. He just has to see us first."

"We're nearly done," said Colby.

And then they heard, "What are you dogs doing? Stop that right now!" shouted Mom.

"Let's go!" said Digger.

"Go, go, go! Hurry, Colby," said Teddi Bear. "Move it." Teddi Bear squeezed out through the hole. Mom was coming fast. "Hurry, Colby," said Teddi Bear again. Colby squeezed through the hole slowly. It was a bit small for him, but he sucked in his tummy just as Mom grabbed a leg.

"Oh, let go," said Colby.

"You come back here!" said Mom.

Colby sucked in his breath again and *pop!* Out went Colby!

Which side do you think Colby ended up on?

Colby popped out with the boys! "Run!" said Colby. "Let's get out of here!" They could hear their mom calling them.

"Come on. Which way to Tyse's house?" asked Digger.

"This way, Digger. I know the way to his house. Wow, that was close," said Colby.

"Is Tyse's house close to us?" asked Digger.

"It's a bit far, but you told us the circus is that way too. We'll be okay," replied Colby. They ran through the neighborhoods, going down one street, up another, and across a few more.

...ey finally got to Tyse's house and looked around for h... ...can't see him," said Digger. "He doesn't seem to be outs... ...ywhere."

...ook," said Teddi Bear. "He's in the window." Tyse spott... ...em and started barking. The boys ducked behind the sh... ...nce around his yard. Tyse's mom opened the front do... ...see what Tyse was barking at. Out Tyse went in a fla... ...fore his mom knew what was happening!

"Tyse! What are you doing?" shouted his mom. "Come back here!"

Tyse, who always listened to his mom's every command, took off like a shot. "Let's go, boys. Let's go," said Tyse as he ran past the others.

mom will chase us in her car! We have to zigzag in
de streets and alleys to lose her, or we won't get
her!" exclaimed Tyse.

e want to get to the circus, we have to move it!"
er.

e going to the circus?" asked Tyse.

bet we are," said Digger. "I think we lost her, an
lose to the circus now."

"Yay, we're here, boys," said Digger.

"Where do we go now?" asked Teddi Bear. "There is so much to see!"

"Well," replied Digger, "I've been here before, and I know that there is a lot of strange stuff going on. I don't think we want to go into the scare houses and weird mirror rooms or anything like that, but there are animals we can look at, and the best place is that big tent right in the middle."

"Wow," said Teddi Bear, "there is so much here and so many people! This is great!"

"Let's go there," said Colby. "There's music and noise and clapping. Let's go see what it's all about!"

"Okay, but we have to sneak in under the tent because they won't let dogs in through the doors," said Digger. "Just find a loose spot in the bottom of the tent, and we can sneak in."

"I found one!" exclaimed Teddi Bear. They all ran to where Teddi Bear was peeking into the tent. His head was in the tent and his bum outside. The other dogs laughed.

Then they all peeked under the tent and were astonished at what they saw.

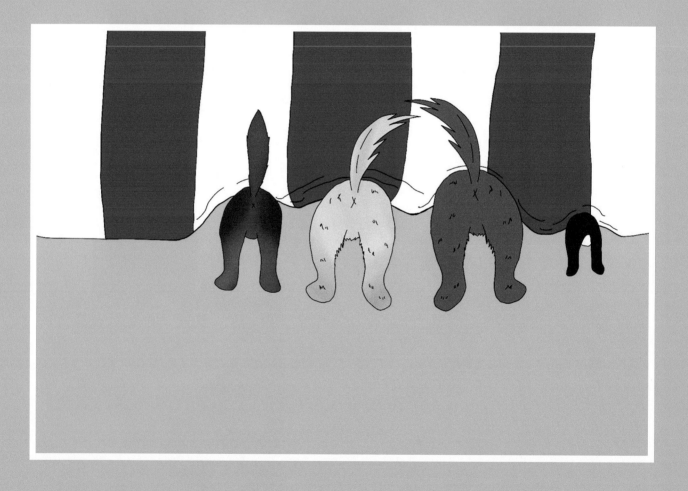

There were so many people sitting on long benches from the ground up, nearly to the top of the tent. There was a man who was dressed funny, announcing something, and beautiful horses running around in a circle. The dogs couldn't believe their eyes!

"[Ha]ve you ever been here before, Tyse?" asked Colby.

"[N]o," replied Tyse. "My mom would never bring me h[ere] [be]cause dogs aren't allowed."

"[We] know," said Colby and Teddi Bear together. "We are[n't] [allo]wed to go either."

"[Bu]t here we are!" exclaimed Digger. "Let's go inside quie[tly] [and] stay on one side to watch what everyone is doing."

They had the horses prancing and dancing around the circle with people doing acrobatics on the horses as they danced.

At the same time, they had acrobats doing all kinds of unbelievable tricks above the dogs on ropes.

Suddenly, someone said, "Let's go, boys. You're on next!" The four dogs looked up at the man, and again, he said, "Let's go. Hurry. You're next!

"You . . . you mean us?" asked Colby, quivering.

"Yes, you. Now get going. You're going to be late!"

The dogs all looked at one another. "Okay," said Digger. "Let's give them a show!"

"Oh, oh," said Colby. They walked around the stands and slowly into the side of the middle ring.

"Wow," exclaimed Tyse. "Look at all the toys here! We're going to have a blast!" The dogs forgot about all the people watching them and started playing with the toys. Tyse found a toy that looked like a balloon that wouldn't break and started poking it with his nose, high into the air over and over again, never dropping it. The crowd was laughing and clapping.

Teddi Bear joined in, then Colby and Digger. All four dogs were bouncing the red toy to one another in turn.

Soon Teddi Bear got bored with the ball and looked around for something else to do. "Hmm, I see a girl riding on a horse. I would like to try that! It looks like fun! Now if I could only find some steps or a platform to get on and jump onto the horse's back as it comes near me. There's one!" exclaimed Teddi Bear. He ran to the platform as fast as he could because the horse and the girl were coming toward the platform.

"Made it!" said Teddi Bear. But the girl jumped off the horse onto the platform. "Hey," said Teddi Bear, but he jumped onto the horse anyway. Away they went, riding around the big top circle. People were laughing and screaming and clapping. They couldn't believe a dog was riding a horse. Teddi Bear was hanging on for dear life.

Colby, Digger, and Tyse were gaping at Teddi Bear. "Do you believe him?" asked Tyse.

"I do," replied Colby. "Our mom always calls him her crazy puppy. He'll be okay." Meanwhile, a bunch of workers were running after the horse, trying to get it to stop. Slowly, the horse stopped, and Teddi Bear jumped down and ran toward the others.

The man who told them to go out into the circle came up to them and said, "That was amazing, boys! What else can you do?" The dogs looked at one another and shrugged their shoulders.

"Let's see what we have to work with, boys," said Digger.

"Can anyone play with a hula hoop? he asked.

"Oh, that's easy," replied Tyse. "I'll take that for a few minutes." Off Tyse went walking and actually twirling the hula hoop around his waist. The crowd cheered and clapped.

Digger asked Colby what he could do. "I don't know," replied Colby. "I used to play like crazy, but when Teddi Bear came home, I kind of stopped playing and watched over him."

"Well, what did you used to like doing?" asked Digger.

"I love playing in water, running, and jumping to catch a whirligig," replied Colby.

"A whirligig?" asked Digger.

"You know that three-sided orange-and-blue thing you throw in the air?" said Colby.

"Oh, like this?" asked Digger, holding up a whirligig.

"Yes, exactly like that," replied Colby

"Okay, go out there and play with it," said Digger

"yay," said Colby. "I haven't done this for a long time."

Out to the ring went Colby with the whirligig in his mouth, trotting with his head high and his tail high and wagging. As soon as Colby got into the ring, he started flipping and tossing the whirligig high in the air and running to catch it. The people laughed and clapped as Colby continued all the way around the tent without dropping it.

When Colby got back to the place where he started tossed the whirligig to Digger. "Your turn, Digger. Wha you going to do?"

"Wow, I don't know. Digging is my specialty, and I don't anyone wants to see that. What can I do? What can I said Digger. "Oh no, oh no, look. Look at the nets under high wire! If someone falls off the high wire or ropes, T Bear will be sent flying high up in the air and off the exclaimed Digger. "How could he possibly get up there

Colby, Digger, and Tyse just stared at Teddi Bear with their mouths hanging open. Everyone in the audience and the performers had stopped everything they were doing and just stared at Teddi Bear bouncing up and down on the net—with a smile on his face.

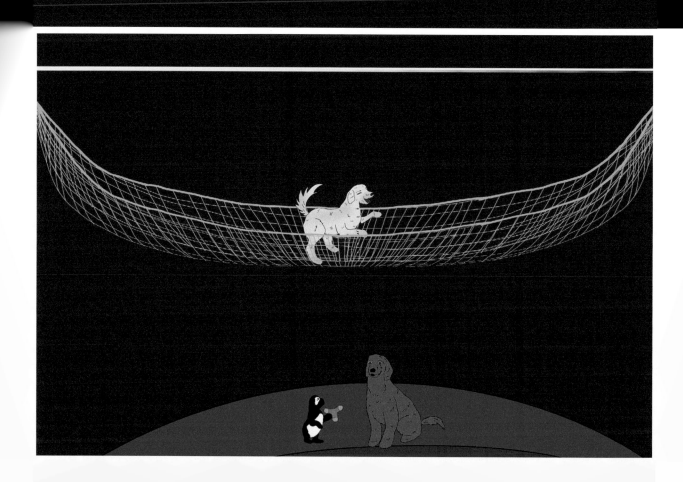

"Oh no, he's going to fall! How did he get there? Someone help him!" the audience was shouting. Teddi Bear was having the time of his life, again. He just kept bouncing on all four feet with a big smile on his face.

Colby yelled at Teddi Bear, "TEDDI BEAR, TEDDI BEAR! GET DOWN FROM THERE! GET DOWN. YOU'RE GOING TO GET HURT! GET DOWN NOW!" Teddi Bear looked down at Colby and saw him yelling something, but he couldn't hear him. Teddi Bear thought Colby looked mad at him or very worried.

"Oh, oh, I think I'm in trouble," he said to himself. Teddi Bear slowly went to the edge of the net and looked down. It was pretty far down. When he got onto the net, a stair truck had been driving close to the net, so he had jumped onto it as the stair truck went by. *No stair truck now! Hmm, what am I going to do now?* he thought.

Actually, I think the boys should come up here too and have some fun!" Teddi Bear didn't think that was going to happe Teddi Bear looked around. How was he going to get down Let's see. There are a bunch of ropes leading down to th ground, but I don't think I can go down a rope. Oh! There a rope ladder! I know how to go up and down a ladder! Mo and Pop used to have a ladder in the pool before they ha the stairs put in. Perfect!

Teddi Bear hopped over to the ladder and grabbed onto it. The crowd became very quiet. *I wonder what is wrong with them,* thought Teddi Bear. *Oh well, here I go!* Teddi Bear slowly went down the ladder. Going up a ladder was easier and this rope ladder was very high and moved when you stepped on it.

Then all of a sudden, Teddi Bear spotted a stair truck coming toward him. "Yay!" said Teddi Bear. He waited for the stair truck, and everyone clapped and cheered. *What is wrong with everyone?* thought Teddi Bear. Then he realized, they were all looking at him. "Ooooh, wow!" Then he waved and barked at everyone. The stair truck stopped below Teddi Bear near him, and he jumped onto the highest stair, and everyone cheered and clapped again. "Oh, wow, again!"

Teddi Bear nodded his head a couple of times as he went down the stairs. Some men were running toward him, so Teddi Bear jumped down and ran to where the other dogs were.

"Run!" he said. So all the dogs ran and hid under the audience stand.

"Teddi Bear," exclaimed Colby, "why did you go up there? You could have fallen and been really injured or worse!"

"Well, I didn't fall," replied Teddi Bear, "and I wanted you guys to come up with me. It was really fun!"

"No way," they replied together.

"Let's sneak out of here from the other side and see what else they have," said Tyse. The dogs slowly crept under the audience stands, and just as Digger (who was leading) went to stick his head out from the stands, a huge foot stomped down right where his head would have been.

"Aaahhh," screamed Digger. "What is that? It nearly squashed my head."

"Wow, that is an elephant," said Colby.

"There are some more! Let's watch this show! Ooh, look, there are some lions and tigers too! Oh, look, there are a bunch of dogs over there playing," exclaimed Teddi Bear. "Let's go play with everyone!" And Teddi Bear started to run toward the lions.

"NO," yelled Colby, and he grabbed Teddi Bear's tail. Screech!

"Hey!" yelled Teddi Bear. "What's wrong? Why did you grab my tail?" he asked.

"Because it is very dangerous to go over there. Those are wild animals," replied Colby. "They are trained, but just with their trainers. They put on a little show, and then they all have to go back into cages. They don't have good lives like we do. Come on, guys. Let's get out of here," said Colby.

"Okay," they all agreed. When the four dogs walked out of the tent, their noses started twitching.

"Oh, boy, something sure smells good around the corner!" exclaimed Digger. "Let's go see what it is."

The dogs ran around the corner and screeched to a stop. "This day just couldn't get any better!" exclaimed Digger. All the dogs were licking their lips. In front of them were all the food stands and trucks. A lot of people were buying all kinds of food.

"Okay," said Teddi Bear. "Food! I am hungry after all that exercise, ha ha."

"Wait," said Digger. "We have to go behind the food tents and trucks and be careful." So the four friends quickly ran to the back of the food places and found all kinds of good food in the garbage and on the ground.

"What is this?" asked Teddi Bear. His face was covered in pink sticky fluff.

"I'm not sure," replied Digger. "Look there's some blue stuff just like it!" Tyse and Digger ran over to the blue fluffy stuff.

"We may not know what it is, but it sure is good!" said Teddi Bear.

Colby took a lick off Teddi Bear's face. "Hey," said Teddi Bear.

Colby laughed. "Ha ha ha, now we both have pink faces." Everyone licked off the sticky stuff and looked around. There were burgers and fries and hot dogs, things on sticks, doughnuts, all kinds of food. They slowly made their way along the back of the food tents and trucks, eating everything they could.

The dogs were so full their tummies bulged!

"Hey, guys, we should go home now," said Colby. "We need to walk off this food. Maybe we can come back another time to see what else they have here and for more good food too! I bet our mom and pop are worried again."

Tyse said, "Yeah, my mom is going to be very worried and mad at me."

"Ours too," chimed in Colby and Teddi Bear. Digger didn't say anything. Only Colby noticed. So Digger and Teddi Bear went bouncing down the street with Colby and Tyse strolling after them.

As they got closer to Tyse's house, they could see his mom sitting on their front steps. She looked so worried! "Oh no," Tyse said. "Bye, guys. Thanks for everything. It was an adventure never to be forgotten." Then he turned and ran to his mom and jumped right on her.

"Oh, Tyse, where have you been?" She hugged him tight, and Tyse licked her. They went into the house.

"Okay, next," said Digger. "We'll take you home this time, Digger." said Colby.

"No, that's okay. You go home. I'm sure your mom and pop are worried about you two. I'm fine."

"Okay," said Colby. "Come on, Teddi Bear. Let's hurry." Colby and Teddi Bear hurried home, still remembering to stop and check for cars before crossing a street.

Finally, they got to their house, and Mom and Pop were sitting on the patio, waiting for them. Oh, they didn't look happy. "Well, at least you aren't as dirty as you were the last time you took off. You still need a bath though. Where on earth do you two go, and why?" Colby barked twice. "How are we going to make sure they don't dig out again?" she asked Pop.

Pop replied, "I don't know, but I'll talk to some people to get some ideas. Let's go, boys, bath time.

"Oh, what is the sticky stuff on their faces?" asked Mom.

"No! They went to the circus. It's candy floss on their faces! I don't believe it! Into the bathroom you go." Colby and Teddi Bear went into the bathroom, had their baths, and Mom called them into the kitchen. She said, "Here is your dinner." Colby and Teddi Bear looked at each other and lay down. There was no way they could eat again. They were so full and so tired they just wanted to sleep. They both put their heads down and went to sleep right away, dreaming about the adventures of the day.

Mom and Pop looked at Colby and Teddi Bear sleeping and said, "Oh! Those crazy dogs!"

Thank you for choosing this book to read. We hope you look forward to book 7 where Colby and Teddi Bear have a visitor!

Books in the Oh! Those Crazy Dogs! series by author CAL

Book 1 *Colby Comes Home*

Book 2 *Teddi Bear Comes Home*

Book 3 *Teddi's First Time at the Cottage*

Book 4 *A New Friend in the Neighborhood! Digger!*

Book 5 *Colby and Teddi Bear Love Swimming in the Pool*

Book 6 *Colby and Teddi Bear Go to the Circus*

Book 7 Coming Soon!

Printed in the United States
by Baker & Taylor Publisher Services